Inside the Web
A Spider Anthology

by Rick McQuiston

Spiders.

The very word sends chills down people's spines. Those creepy little bugs that crawl along on eight legs, their eight eyes gyrating in every direction, the fine hairs on their bodies bristling in the breeze as they silently and viciously stalk their prey, are for some people the stuff of nightmares.

I have a great fear of spiders myself, which I suppose is why I choose to write about them. Since they frighten me I find it relatively easy to create a good scary story about them.

So here I offer you, brave reader, a dozen of my tales on the nasty little, eight-legged critters, all geared toward keeping you up at night and checking under the sheets before you climb into bed.

So please, light a blood-red candle, pour yourself a hot cauldron of tea, and be careful that you don't find yourself *Inside the Web*.

Rick

CONTENTS

The Spider

The spider was perfectly motionless. During its short life it had managed to perfect the art of concealment and camouflage; they were necessary attributes for its survival. Its prey was intelligent, and usually quite adept at eluding the spider's grasp, and it knew this all too well. Many times it had lost a potential meal, too many for its liking.

Vague memories floated about in the spider's tiny, fragile brain, occasionally converging to form a coherent collage of past events capable of recognition, and in some cases reflection.

The thought of its last meal, a rather plump housefly that fought valiantly right up until the moment of injection, strayed across the spider's mind. It had apparently become injured while flying into a small window. Obviously it thought it was an open pathway to greener pastures.

But that had been quite a while ago. Too many midnights had passed since the fly succumbed to its venom.

Pangs of hunger relentlessly tapped into the spider's mind, attempting to shatter its delicate grip on life. The strange sensations it had been experiencing also reasserted themselves, further adding to the spider's discomfort. The beakers of liquid it stumbled across in the back room of the house had hardly proved to be an adequate quencher of its thirst, a fact that the spider was becoming all too familiar with. It thought they had contained water but it discovered that that was far from the truth.

Still, the fluids were intoxicating, almost to the point of being addictive, and although its thirst and hunger were still raging, it did feel somewhat rejuvenated.

The spider recalled others like itself in the back room as well. Some were large and hairy, and others were small, but all were housed inside various-sized bottles with wide labels attached to them.

Black Widow (Latrodectus mactans), Northern Funnel Web (Atrax robustus), and Brazilian Wanderer (Phoneutria nigriventer) were but a few of the specimens inside the room.

The spider also noticed several small mice in glass boxes on the tables. It could not reach them however because they were surrounded by much equipment.

The spider's stomach began to contort. The cat it had swallowed had been digested and it now had all of its eyes focused on the family dog. It was a large dog, much bigger than the cat, but the spider did not care, hunger directed its actions.

It pounced on the poor creature in a flash and greedily sucked down the corpse.

The spider was surprised that its hunger still was not satisfied. It wondered in its mutating and rapidly-expanding brain what it had drunk in the back room of the house. The complex neurotoxin dripping from its expanding fangs occasionally dribbled onto its own legs, causing necrotic lesions, but it did not care, the pain was minimal compared to its hunger.

The spider was barely able to squeeze through the doorway but finally managed to do it. It sensed food nearby and an obstacle like a wall or a door was not about to stop it.

It entered the room and quickly squatted behind a large couch, attempting to hide itself. But it was no good, it was far too big. So it instead opted for a swift, violent attack instead of a slow, calculated one.

The little girl sat in front of the television, unaware that she was being watched. She was singing along to her favorite program while eating the ham sandwich her mother had made for her. She was also looking forward to that evening when her daddy promised her he would play tea party with her. He was always so busy in his laboratory that he usually didn't have much time for her or her mommy, but she knew the work he was doing was very important and that it would save lives one day.

The spider's fangs drooled in anticipation. It watched the little girl closely, waiting for the opportunity to strike. The hunger it was feeling was maddening, prohibiting it from applying patience to its hunt. It knew it would have to attack soon…very soon.

The little girl's mother strolled into the living room to see if her daughter wanted something else to eat.

She screamed when she saw the half-eaten ham sandwich lying in front of the television…covered in blood.

*   *   *   *

The cockroach squeezed through the tiny hole in the wall. It was hungry and desperately needed to find food.

The room was very strange; there were many containers with spiders in them, and small mice in glass cages as well.

It entered the room cautiously, being driven by its desire for food. The thirst it suffered from was also strong, and it was pleased to find some glass containers with liquid in them.

It scurried over to them it began to lap up the water.

And then it realized it was not water.

Do You Love Me?

When Austin woke up his head felt as if someone had cut it off and used it to play basketball with. A migraine would have been an improvement.

He stood up and rubbed his eyes until the room came into focus, trying his best to ignore the throbbing in his skull.

Foggy but persistent memories from the night before filtered into his already confused mind. He remembered hanging out near the highway with his best friend Ray, waiting for their dates to show up.

Tammy was Ray's girl. She was short and petite with a full head of blond curls and a lively personality to match. They really got along well, so well in fact that they had even started talking about marriage.

Angela was his date. She was a thin beauty with a silken mane of flowing jet- black hair framing her face perfectly.

He knew he was falling in love with her, although he hadn't worked up the nerve to tell her yet. In his life, rejection was often a painful consequence of impatience and foolishness, a consequence he had unfortunately experienced before.

Ray had introduced them during a party at his house. He discovered she had two daughters, Eve and Kate, and they were the spitting image of their mother, sharing her gentle personality and sweet, enticing smile. Normally he tried to stay away from women with children, but in Angela's case he found himself making an exception.

As the room came into focus he was able to fully understand his predicament, and it was as confusing as it was frightening.

He was in a large, empty room with walls made of some type of metal and painted a featureless gray, as was the ceiling and floor. He didn't see any windows or source of light, despite the fact that the room was illuminated well enough for him to see. He was all alone with nothing but cobwebs to keep him company.

But one thing did catch his attention: the doors. Or more accurately: the outline of two doors on the far wall.

Although they didn't appear to be doors. They were not made of wood or metal, but of the same material as the walls, and the hinges and knobs were so faint he had trouble seeing them. They were only thin, nearly-imperceptible lines framing the curious openings.

He stood up and waited for his head to stop spinning, knowing his options were limited. Without thinking, he let loose several shouts for help and hearing no response, approached one of the doors.

There were two of them, identical in shape and size, separated about five feet from each other.

He bent over and examined one of the doors in closer detail. What he saw sent waves of confusion and fear through his body.

The doorknob and hinges were made of cobwebs!

Too afraid to think, he reached out and touched the handle. It felt solid enough but in a surrealistic type of way.

It could be a way out. It could lead to safety.

He started to turn the knob.

But it could also lead to certain death...or worse.

He released the handle.

The dwindling options available to him danced around in his head. Should he try to open the doors or simply sit back and wait for help? Neither choice was too appealing, but he realized that sooner or later he would have to do something.

Fear eventually won out and he flopped to the floor with his eyes glued to the doors for any signs of danger. His head still ached and he could only pray he wouldn't pass out, although sleep was appearing more and more attractive by the minute.

Eventually he dozed off.

She came to him in a dream. Her piercing eyes entranced him as her silky jet-black hair swirled all around, wrapping him up in its delicate embrace.

"Austin," the dream voice asked. "Do you love me?"

"Yes," he heard himself say as if he were separated from his body. "Yes, I do love you."

A short pause was immediately followed by a soft giggle.

"Good. Very good," the dream voice said. "I will see you very soon, my love. Very soon."

Austin jerked awake and rubbed his swollen eyes. The strange dream had taken its toll on him, further weakening his frail condition. He knew waiting for help was fast becoming an option he couldn't afford much longer.

The two doorknobs gradually came into view. He stood up and stumbled over to one of them, ignoring the voice of reason in his head. He must try to escape or he would surely die.

A dry creak echoed in the room as the door swung open, revealing a solid wall of darkness behind it.

"Hello? Is there anybody in there?" he asked, not particularly anxious for a response.

Silence.

He began to close the door when a small, almost indecipherable sound stirred in the darkness. It sounded like someone, or something, drinking.

And then he noticed a pair of eyes.

They shone with the reflection from the room behind him and were unblinking. And worst of all…they were looking directly at him. Six more eyes then joined the first two and immediately focused on him.

An outline of something the size of a basketball was lying on the ground approximately ten feet away from him. His stomach convulsed when he realized it was a head, a human head…Ray's head. Or more accurately, what was left of it.

Stumbling backward, he kicked the door shut with all of the strength he had left. Whatever was beyond the door pushed up against it violently, causing terrible sounds that reverberated throughout the room.

Thinking quickly, he brushed away the cobwebs lining the doors, thus erasing them from existence.

Standing back, he surveyed the now empty wall. It was as plain as it had been when he had awoken in the room, but the thought of what might be trapped behind it frightened him beyond words. The crashing noises had subsided, but the ghosts of their echoes still rung in his ears. He fell to the ground yet again, a victim of exhaustion and hunger, and passed into an uneasy sleep.

When he woke up all was quiet. He reached up to rub his eyes and realized that he could hardly move his arms. Something bound them in place in his lap. He tried to break free but his weakened condition simply would not allow it. And then he noticed what was holding him down: cobwebs.

"Austin, do you love me?" the familiar voice asked.

"Angela? Is that you?"

"Do you love me?" it repeated.

"Angela, get me outta here!"

"DO…YOU…LOVE…ME!"

He didn't want to answer; it might make his already dire situation even worse.

And then he made the mistake of looking up. Cobwebs were gathering together right before his eyes. He watched in horror as they began to drift down into the room. Their descent was fluid and smooth, but with purpose, and eventually they settled on the opposite wall, forming the outline of a door.

His stomach was in knots. He knew what was happening to some degree but not how, or more importantly, why. He also knew whatever was behind that door was probably going to be very happy to see him…but in the wrong way. He rolled over onto his side and frantically tore into his bonds, but they felt like steel cables.

And then he looked up again.

Three more strands of cobwebs were drifting down from above. Two thinned out and turned vertically, and one rolled up into a ball. He knew right away what they were: hinges and a doorknob.

In seconds they had attached themselves to the door.

Further attempts to dislodge himself only succeeded in tightening the cobwebs even more, and they were fastening to the floor, leaving him more vulnerable than ever.

The door creaked as it opened, filling the room with its threatening echo. Austin could only crane his neck to one side, which was not enough to look away from the door.

"Austin, do you love me?" Angela's voice asked from the black void.

His mouth was the only part of his body not covered with cobwebs, a fact that didn't go unnoticed by him.

"I...I can't move. Please let me go," he pleaded.

Something massive shifted in the darkness. It was confident in its strength.

"It would be better if you told me that you loved me," Angela's voice slurred. "So much better. You would taste so much better."

"Angela, pleeeeaase! Let me go."

He could only pray for it to be quick, struggling to think of happier times. Times when he was a young boy frolicking around in his backyard. Times like hitting his first home run, or having his first kiss. Times like hanging out with his friends...friends like Ray who was now undoubtedly in the belly of some inhuman thing behind a non-existent door made of cobwebs! And he could also still hear the things slamming against the wall where the other doors had been. He surmised that little Kate and Eve were still very hungry, even after they had finished with Ray and Tammy.

He focused on the black square of darkness behind the large door. The face that was beginning to materialize from the darkness was growing larger by the second.

Eventually, its visage was clear.

It was Angela.

In a way, Austin felt relieved to see her, although he knew it wasn't the same girl he had been dating.

She glared at him with four pairs of baby-blue eyes, conflicting sharply with their real intent.

Austin's heart was in his throat when Angela scuttled out into the open room.

"Hello Austin," she hissed through nine-inch fangs.

"Angela?"

"Yes, it's me," she answered while straddling him with her eight hairy legs. "Did you miss me?" The mockery in her words was plainly evident and stung him like a needle.

Despite his situation, despite what she really was, Austin could not deny to himself that he had loved her, that he still loved her. Perhaps that was why she had kept him around for so long. Maybe her past boyfriends, her other meals, had never truly loved her. It was possible that she had never experienced actual love before and was having difficulty dealing with it.

He knew it was his only chance.

"Angela, I know you're in there," he moaned to the creature. "I can feel it. Tell me it's really you."

Angela paused for a moment, pondering Austin's words. The inner conflict in her mind was reflected on her face.

"Austin, do you love me?"

A tear welled in Austin's eye. His heart ached for the creature to be Angela again, to be the woman he loved.

"Y…yes Angela, I love you," he managed to whisper.

The sharp pain in his side was causing him to become disoriented, but he wanted to say the words before he blacked out. They just might save his life.

"Yes Angela, I love you," he managed to whisper.

And then his world went dark.

Angela squatted back on her bloated abdomen and gazed down at Austin. She had truly loved him and she knew it. But she also knew that one needed more than love to survive. One also needed food.

She clicked her fangs together and waited for the venom to begin its work.

There's a Killer in the House

Paige just couldn't shake the feeling that she was being watched. It clung to her like a bad hairdo.

Jerry Fizzeral, the creepy guy who was stationed in the cubicle next to hers, had been fired that morning for using his computer to research how to make pipe bombs of all things. The management staff zeroed in on it pretty quickly, and when he was confronted he merely stated that it was a hobby he was interested in.

A hobby? Pipe bombs? Who did he think he was kidding?

In any event, he was let go immediately and received a stern warning not to come back onto the property, even to get his last check. They told him they would mail it to him.

To say she was relieved he was gone was a vast understatement. Just the thought that she wouldn't have to see those beady little eyes or that crooked smile again was cause for celebration.

And that was just one of the interesting things that had happened during her day.

On her way home she had stopped to get her dry cleaning and who of all people did she run into: her beloved ex-boyfriend Sam. He strolled into the store and sauntered right up next to her. He claimed that he was just picking up his clothes, but she knew the real story. He had stalked her before. Fortunately for her he didn't follow her when she quickly departed the store.

And then there was the weirdo who had followed her car practically to her own driveway. He had tailgated her in his big black truck while sporting a grin that sent chills down her spine. She contemplated calling the police but he hadn't actually done anything, at least not yet.

When she walked in her front door she felt like she was going to collapse. All she wanted to do was flop in front of the fireplace with a hot cup of tea.

There's a killer in the house.

The unsettling phrase crept into her mind, refusing to relinquish its hold on her imagination.

Was she being watched?

She didn't think so, but one could never be sure. She lifted her cup of Lemon-Ginseng tea out of the microwave and settled down in front of the fireplace. The flames crackled and popped, radiating their warmth into the room.

There's a killer in the house.

It was no use. No matter how hard she tried to relax she couldn't ignore the feeling she was having. The best thing to do would be to make sure there was no one in the house with her. She set her cup of tea down on the coffee table and pushed the afghan off of her lap.

And then she hesitated.

She had neglected to turn on any lights before she had sat down and now the house was brimming with shadows.

The irrationality of being so frightened in her own home weighed heavy on her mind. She was a grown woman, independent and intelligent. She owned her own house, a new car, and had a moderately-sized investment portfolio. There was no reason to be afraid, none whatsoever.

There's a killer in the house.

Except for that.

That and the movement she thought she detected in the guest bathroom at the end of the hallway.

It was difficult to steady her nerves, much less face her fears, but she had to do it. What other choice did she have?

Was it that creep Fizzeral? Did he find out that she had been the one who had told on him at work? Maybe he had gotten her address from the computers before he left and was waiting for her to get home. Who knows what terrible things he had planned for her. She could just picture those beady eyes and that crooked smile sneering at her in the shadows.

She picked up the fireplace poker and held it out in front like a sword.

"Who's there?" she called out. "I'm armed and able to defend myself."

But there was no reply.

Without thinking, she rushed straight to the bathroom and flicked on the light.

It was only a towel that was hanging in the path of the heat register. When the furnace kicked on it blew air on it, obviously causing the movement she had seen.

The relief she felt was like a tidal wave. It washed over her completely, cleansing her of her paranoia. She settled back down to her cup of tea, being sure to leave some lights on this time.

The scratching noise jarred her from her relaxation. It sounded as if someone was outside the kitchen window trying to get in. She bolted to her feet, again wielding the poker in front of her.

Could it be Sam? She'd caught him outside her house twice before after they'd broken up. He had said both times that he only wanted to make sure she was all right and that he still cared for her. She didn't buy any of it though. He was a louse, and a jealous, stalking one at that.

Moonlight filtered into the kitchen, casting an eerie glow on the granite countertop and appliances. She was afraid to go near the window, fearing that Sam was lurking beyond the glass with a knife or gun. His jealousy only served to enhance his temper, as she had found out many times in the past. When she noticed the small bird pecking at the glass near the bottom of the window the relief she felt nearly caused her to collapse. A sudden tap on the windowpane quickly removed the pest from her sight and her mind.

Again she settled back to her cup of tea, which was now starting to cool. She let her mind stray, delving into fond, distant memories of her childhood.

There's a killer in the house.

The phrase corrupted her peace and quiet, firmly implanting itself in her mind, refusing to fade away. She couldn't ignore it, it was incessant, and addressing it seemed liked a childish and fruitless endeavor. When she had sensed things in the past she was usually right about them, so she was hesitant to ignore these particular words.

The doorbell caused her heart to skip a beat. She jumped up out of her seat and scurried to the front door. Cautiously, she peered out the small window at the top of the door, being sure not to be seen.

Nobody was there.

And then she noticed the black truck parked across the street.

An ice-cold shiver ran down her spine.

Was that weird guy who followed her home stalking her? Was he playing mind games with her? She locked the deadbolt and gripped the poker tightly.

After she had taken three steps toward the phone the doorbell shattered the silence. She paced back to the door, this time fully prepared to defend herself.

The back truck was still there, although she knew it wasn't the cause of her worry. As she watched in relief, the big man who was driving it earlier emerged from her neighbor's house carrying a large television set. Her neighbor, a woman she'd seen countless times before but had never actually gotten to know very well, followed behind him carrying a VCR machine. They proceeded to load the pieces into the back of the truck. The man then gave her neighbor some cash and they shook hands before he drove off.

A rustling in the bushes alerted her to the cause of the doorbell ringing. Two small boys ran off when they noticed the victim of their practical joke had spotted them.

She let a soft chuckle escape when she realized just how ridiculous she had been. There was no killer in the house. She was all alone.

There's a killer in the house.

The ominous words attempted to take control of her mind as they had done before. But this time she wasn't going to listen to them. There was nobody in the house besides her. She had checked it thoroughly. This time she was going to listen to her common sense.

She removed the coffee cup from the microwave and dipped her finger in the water. Satisfied that it was hot enough she put a new tea bag into the cup and sat back down to relax.

There's a killer in the house.

Forget it. Sorry. Not this time. This time she was going to enjoy the rest of her night. Her favorite show was due to come on shortly and she fully intended to watch it.

She set her cup of tea down on the end table and reached for the remote control, not noticing the Black Widow spider crouched next to it, ready to strike.

Web

Luke reached up a shaking hand and felt for the knot on his forehead. It only took him a few seconds to find it. He gasped at its size and how tender it was.

A lone figure materialized out of the darkness and handed him something. "I think you'll need these."

Luke blinked a dozen times to clear his foggy vision. He took the glasses and put them on. Instantly, the figure came into focus.

Louise sat down next to the bed. "You gave me a scare there, Luke." She brushed aside her long black hair. A few strands refused to stay off her pretty face.

Luke sat up in bed. "You know, when we bought this old place, I had no idea that it would fight back."

"Oh, you're just being silly," Louise said softly. She held Luke's hand, gently caressing his palm with her thumb. "It's just an old house. It has a lot of character. That's one of the things we liked about it, remember?"

"Yeah, I remember. I just didn't know it would be so painful."

"Very funny. What happened down there anyway?"

Luke saw a damp washcloth next to the bed and carefully laid it on the egg-sized bump on his head. "I don't know exactly. One minute I was walking down to the cellar with some boxes of vegetables, and the next minute I was sprawled out on the floor. Maybe I didn't see a board in the ceiling or something."

Louise stood up. "When I found you, you were mumbling something about a web. And I found the boxes, but they were empty."

"A web, really?"

"Really."

"All right, if you say so."

Louise nodded thoughtfully. She wished she could stay with her husband, but she had to go to work. "Well, Honey, I have to get going. Now I want you to get some rest."

Luke smiled and closed his eyes.

"Good. I'll be back by seven, okay? Love you."

"Love you too."

*   *   *   *

The cellar was dark and smelled musty. The steps wound away from the top floor like frightened children escaping a stranger's grasp. A solitary light bulb, unlit and dust-covered, hung from a single wire at the base of the stairway.

Luke stood in the doorway. He gazed down at the lower level of his new house and shuddered. As a kid, he had a bad experience in a cellar once: the door locked behind him and he was trapped for over an hour.

When he ventured down into the cellar earlier, he was so busy unpacking he didn't give it a second thought. But after he passed out it brought back those old childhood fears again.

What did he hit his head on? Was it really a low rafter like he was trying to convince himself of? Or was it what he vaguely remembered: some type of web? And furthermore, what happened to the vegetables?

"Luke, you're an adult now. You have to behave like one." He began to step down into the cellar. "You just bumped your head on a board." The steps creaked and groaned under his weight. "Just a board."

Luke never saw it coming. The pencil-thin strand was stretched across the foot of the stairs, from one support beam to another. There was no slack in. It was so taut it could've cut through a slab of cheese.

Luke fell to the floor, and hovered between blacking out and a fuzzy awareness of his surroundings. His forehead where the strand hit sported a deep-red furrow. Blood seeped from the wound.

Time slowed, refusing to allow itself to be measured accurately. The room distorted. Light traded places with darkness, and then back again. And a pair of eyes, blood-red and diagonally elliptical, emerged from the dust-coated rafters.

Luke watched helplessly as the gigantic spider lowered its massive bulk to the cellar's floor. It was wedged in between the rafter boards so effectively it was nearly invisible; its deep brown hide meshed in perfectly with its surroundings; its foot-long fangs clicked against one another.

It was hungry; the vegetables it had eaten hardly satisfied its appetite. Now it had overcome its initial fear of the creature that had been carrying them. Now it was ready for a real meal.

The spider scrambled over and crouched above Luke. Its bloated abdomen pinned him to the ground. It reached up and effectively snipped its web strand, rolling it into a tight ball which it tossed out of the way.

Luke looked up at the underside of the beast. If he could've screamed, he would have done so like never before.

He never saw the fangs coming.

*   *   *   *

Louise pulled the door shut behind her and immediately noticed how quiet the house was. The ticking of a clock on the wall sounded like a jackhammer in church. She set her purse down and slipped off her shoes.

"Luke? I'm home. Luke?"

No answer. Only silence filled the house.

As she walked toward the kitchen, quietly scolding herself for being so paranoid, Louise noticed the cellar door was open.

No, it wasn't just open, it was damaged. The whole framework looked as if something too big to fit forced its way past it, pushing the jam boards out in the process. The door itself hung precariously at a downward angle toward the steps.

"Luke? Are you down there?"

Still no reply.

Louise reached in and flipped the light switch on. Instantly, the light at the foot of the stairs came on. She screamed when she saw the sucked-dry husk of her husband.

All she could think about was getting out of the house. She turned and sprinted down the hallway, bumping into the walls as she went. A framed photograph of her and Luke on their honeymoon crashed to the floor. An antique lamp toppled from its base on a small table.

"I got to get my cell phone! No, get out of the house! I'll need my car keys! No... my purse! I have to get out of the house!"

The front door loomed in front of Louise. She stumbled toward it, all the while trying her best to block out the image of Luke's body.

The strand of web cut so deeply into her stomach it knocked the breath out of her. She wound up flat on the floor of the hallway, not more than four feet from the front door.

Gasping for breath, Louise watched as the giant spider crammed its massive bulk through the archway from the kitchen. It was able to shift its exoskeleton, allowing it to approach its prey with relative ease.

The last thought Louise had was that she hated spiders.

    *   *   *   *

The mail truck rolled down the long dirt driveway. Annie held the day's mail in her hand. She eyed the mailbox on its wooden pole near the entrance to the house, and was about to come to a stop next to it when something caught her attention, something that told her to call the police.

The front door of the house was smashed open. It looked as if something big had forced its way through the opening. Splinters of wood were scattered in all directions.

Annie fumbled for her cell phone, but was knocked forward when the mail truck suddenly hit something. It bobbed up and down a few times, dangling off the ground. The strand of web had cut right through the top of the truck, holding it fast.

Annie rubbed her eyes as she tried to orient herself. Her forehead was bleeding and her wrist hurt. She looked up and noticed the windshield was cracked.

And through the cracked glass she saw the enormous spider lumbering toward her.

In the Folds

The spider did its to best avoid falling into the crevice but couldn't stop its descent. Its jet-black body gently slid into the folds of the blanket, coming to rest between soft comforter on one side and a heaving mass of human on the other.

Even though it was covered by the blanket, the human's sheer size, compared to the spider's, was frightening. If it could have comprehended fear better the spider would have scurried away. But instead, it merely settled down in the folds and waited.

*   *   *   *

Jimmy rolled over in bed and instantly his young mind began to race with the upcoming day's activities.

The birthday party, *his* birthday party, was going to be great. His mom promised him lots of presents and games, and even hinted at the possibility of a magician.

Jimmy could hardly contain his excitement. He got dressed and went into the bathroom to brush his teeth.

As foamy toothpaste dribbled down his chin, Jimmy felt a sudden ache in his stomach. It was strange, like a stone sitting in his gut, hard and pressing against the delicate lining.

He began to panic, but suppressed the urge. He was a big boy now, having just turned eight, and he had to be strong. And besides, he wasn't going to let a stomachache ruin his party.

But the stone sat there in his gut, immovable and yet somehow…

alive?

The word frightened him. He knew it was impossible, but he still felt worried.

He left the bathroom without another thought about it.

Eventually though, Jimmy couldn't ignore the discomfort any longer. As he sat in the kitchen, deciding what to have for breakfast, he clutched his stomach and fell to the floor. The pain wracked his body, sending red-hot tendrils to every part, every limb.

And they all spread out from one central spot: his stomach.

"Mom!" he cried out. "Mom! Help!"

Jimmy slipped in and out of consciousness. The pain in his stomach twisted him around like a rag doll, pulling him into darkness, only to push him back to the light of day again.

Jocelyn raced into the kitchen. The feeling she felt when she saw her little boy on the floor was beyond anything she could comprehend. It was like someone slamming a sledgehammer into her gut.

She dropped to the floor next to her son, and cradling his head in one arm, fumbled for her cell phone with the other.

She managed to punch in the first number:

nine.

She tapped the second number:

one.

But before she could dial the third number, something caught her eye, something that should not be, but was.

Her boy, her precious little boy wasn't moving. He lay there, sprawled out on the kitchen floor, apparently dead. He was completely still, except...

except for a delicate movement near his stomach.

Jocelyn recoiled in horror when she saw something begin to stretch the fabric of Jimmy's shirt. It pushed upward, bringing the fabric to a sharp point. Inevitably, the shirt then tore open as a leg, a jet-black spider's leg the size of a man's arm, rose up from the gaping wound. A head followed immediately after, and focusing on the screaming woman nearby, the spider lunged out of the corpse and shot straight for her mouth.

Things that Bite

Tiffany felt a cold shiver slide up and down her spine. She gripped the dull steak knife in her sweaty hand, trying desperately to extract any confidence she could from the makeshift weapon.

But she didn't feel confident. She felt scared. Scared for her life; scared for the life of her unborn child; scared for whoever was still alive outside the walls of the dilapidated house she was holed up in.

It was late, probably past 5 a.m. if she had to guess, and she was anxious to see the sun rise above the horizon. If nothing else it would at least make her feel better. She would know then that there was hope, a chance, however small it may be.

But she didn't expect to see the sun. The past three days it hadn't made an appearance. No life-giving globe bathing the landscape with warm light; no spirit-lifting sign from God Himself that the human species would continue.

With a heavy heart, Tiffany looked down at the knife in her hand. It felt too light, so much so that it might've been nothing at all. With such a poor excuse for a weapon she'd only be able to kill one, maybe two of the spiders at a time. That, surely, wouldn't be enough to guarantee her survival. Not by a long shot.

But it was all she had.

To her left, on the floor and not more than ten feet away, one of the beasts was sprawled out in its own gore. A thick, pasty soup of arachnid innards coated the remains, rendering the unusually large spider virtually unrecognizable. Only its eight spindly legs, curled upward above its squashed body like some crazy decorative sculpture, gave clue to what it used to be.

Tiffany ran her fingers through the matted tufts of her strawberry-blonde curls. Her hair used to be so pretty, so soft and easy to manage. Now, thanks to nearly a week of being trapped in a godforsaken house with hardly any food and no means of keeping her personal hygiene intact, her once beautiful head of hair resembled substrate from an aquarium floor.

She forced her weakened body up off the floor and stepped over to the dead spider.

It was large, over a foot and a half across, and had eyes (what was left of them) the size of golf balls.

One still glared up at her from its oozing eye socket.

She recoiled from the sight of it.

"Why are you so big?" she asked the lifeless mess. "And why are you so aggressive?"

The spider did not answer.

Tiffany stood up and stretched her aching back. A series of pops and cracks echoed in the room, eliciting groans of satisfaction from her.

A boarded up window dominated a dust-coated wall.

She hoped that the boards would hold.

She looked to her left.

The spiders had been everywhere, a seething carpet of thrashing fangs and writhing legs, a veritable onslaught of things that bite. They had blanketed the town like a disease.

Tiffany had barely managed to avoid getting bitten. How, she wasn't sure, but she had made it through town without any significant injury other than an aching feeling in her chest from the exertion.

"God, if only I had my phone," she lamented. "If only I had some way to call for help."

She stumbled across the room. The wall kept her from falling, and she braced herself against it, marveling in her thirst and hunger-induced state of mind how it felt. Similar to padded carpet, the drywall yielded to her probing fingers like a slightly damp sponge would.

Tiffany, disoriented from her harrowing ordeal, moved away from the wall. She felt as if there were dozens, hundreds of hairy legs brushing against her body.

She heard a noise behind her. It was vague, yet distinct, distant and yet familiar.

Whirling around, she saw something that was so impossible it froze the blood in her veins.

A leg, a multi-segmented, hairy leg was protruding out of the wall. It had a girth the size of a broomstick handle and was a foot long, perhaps more. Spiny black and brown- colored hairs bristled on the horrible thing as it moved.

Tiffany was transfixed at the sight. A knot formed in her gut, churning in the juices like a stone would in the rapids.

The leg bent forward until it found purchase on the wall. It positioned itself accordingly, and pressed down, effectively gaining leverage as it began to help the body it was attached to free itself from its impossible confines.

Another leg then poked out of the wall just below the first one.

And then another.

And yet another.

And then more, four more to be exact, each and every one similar in size, shape, and disposition to the first one.

At that moment, more than any other time since the nightmare began, Tiffany's world crumbled. Before, the spiders, the absence of daylight, the hopelessness of being trapped and alone in an abandoned house, the hunger and thirst, she had bared it all. But this: huge spiders actually crawling out of walls, this was too much for her to endure.

She felt her sanity slipping away.

"I need to defend myself," she said to no one, as if hearing the words somehow validated them. "I'm not going to die in the stinking place!" She pointed at the wall where there were now more spiders oozing forward. "You hear me, you freaks! I'm not going to die here!"

The outburst gave Tiffany a surge of energy, albeit temporary and somewhat minor. But she embraced it nonetheless. It energized her resolve.

Soon, the entire wall was squirming with life. Dozens of cat-sized spiders filled every square inch of the wall, writhing in every direction like stranded fish on a beach.

Tiffany realized what was happening. It both scared and terrified her; she struggled to remain standing.

The house wasn't real. None of it was. It was some kind of crazy imitation, a façade, a fake.

She looked at her hand, just below the palm, near her thumb. A pair of tiny, identical points of red gazed up at her like a set of angry eyes.

I was bitten. I didn't make it through town without being injured. One of them must have got me when I wasn't looking.

The venom in her system had spread quickly. Its complex neurotoxins rendered her grasp of reality hazy at best, hallucinatory at worst.

The spiders began to crawl down the wall. Their myriad eyes were focused on Tiffany, reflecting evil beyond their ability to feel such emotions. But they did feel such evil, and it directed every move they made.

Tiffany's hand was throbbing. Why the venom had such a delayed reaction she couldn't explain, but it was now making itself known to the full extent of its potency.

She fell to the floor, cradling her rapidly-swelling hand to her chest.

A large spider scuttled up to her. Its fangs clicked against one another. Its bulbous abdomen jostled from side to side. Its legs seemingly moved in slow motion.

"Get away from me!" Tiffany cried as she swung the knife in a deadly arc.

The blade sliced across one of the spider's legs, neatly severing the hairy limb. A glob of pus-colored goo pooled at the bloody stump.

The beast reared back on its haunches and thrashed wildly, spewing blood in all directions. The spiders around it were splashed with the gore but didn't seem to care. They continued to crawl forward.

Tiffany forced herself to her feet and stumbled backward.

She reached back for support from anything she could find: a table; a chair; a wall, anything that would help her maintain her balance as she kept her eyes on the things in front of her.

Her hand brushed against a lamp. The shade touched her wrist and instantly shot a lightning bolt of white-hot pain up her arm.

Did something bite me?

She looked around and saw a pair of red dots on her skin.

But she didn't cry out. Instead, she bit her lip so hard it bled. If she made any sudden movements the spiders might react and pounce on her. If she kept her cool and maintained the slow steady withdrawal from the room, she'd at least have a chance.

Her head ached. Slivers of pain coursed through her, making it very difficult to remain calm.

She moved her hand away from the lamp.

~ 38 ~

She carefully slipped the knife into her back pocket and reached for the wall behind her.

She felt the wall.

It felt…

hairy?

Off to her right a large spider hissed.

She turned her head.

It was bright orange with blue stripes on its legs and the size of a fully grown dog. A bald patch on its abdomen indicated generous use of its urticating hairs in the past.

"Get away. Keep away from me."

The spider inched forward. Three others of similar size and coloration soon joined it.

The arachnid battalion focused on its prey.

Tiffany lifted her hand and looked at the puncture wounds. They were swollen with infection and throbbed.

The venom. That's what is creating this mess I'm in. It's the cause of it.

She pushed her mouth against the bite area and started to suck out the poison. Instantly, a bitter fluid reminiscent of spoiled milk seeped into her mouth.

She spat it out.

The spiders crept forward. They hissed and jostled for position with each other.

Time slowed. A deathly silence drifted down. The air became thick with tension.

Tiffany fell to the floor and closed her eyes as tightly as she could. She tried to slip back to a time when she was a little girl, a time when something scared her she would just close her eyes and wish it away. Back then, when life was simple, it always seemed to work, an easy way to chase away demons.

But this time she knew it wouldn't work. The spider's venom was altering her perception of reality somehow. Or perhaps it wasn't only her perception of reality, but reality itself that was being altered. Maybe they weren't really spiders after all, or at least none that any scientist had ever classified before. Maybe they had the ability to change reality, to bend the rules, to make things more to their liking.

Like transforming things such as walls and lamps into…into…

The realization of what was happening struck Tiffany like a freight train.

"No…no, it can't be. It can't be."

She turned and stumbled on a tattered old rug. Her foot caught one of the folds and down she went, crashing to the dusty floor like a tree felled by lumberjacks.

She looked at the rug and noticed that it had legs, eight legs to be precise, hairy, multi-jointed things that were bright orange with blue stripes.

And as she stared, a pair of eyes emerged near the edge of the rug, followed by three more pairs of eyes. The rug then lifted, forming a small cave-like opening where two glistening fangs curved downward. Droplets of milky venom dripped from the tip of each one.

Tiffany scuttled away from the thing, from the rug that was alive. It snapped at her, its fangs narrowly missing her feet.

A fang did snag her pants however, slicing the fabric open with ease.

She backed up against a wall and pulled the knife from her pocket, waving it in the air. But her threatening gesture didn't deter the advance of the spiders.

With caution thrown to the wind she hurled the knife at a nearby window. At the very least she wanted to see the sun one more time before she died.

The blade collided with the aged, fragile window with a sickening thud as glass shattered in a maelstrom of jagged shards. Hundreds of fragments crashed to the ground. Many more remained embedded along the rusted frame of the window.

The first thing that registered in Tiffany's clouded-over mind was the obvious absence of wind. The rectangular opening stood before her like a smattering of jet-black paint against an otherwise unfinished canvas.

And, as she already expected, no sun. Nothing but a black chasm, void of light or life.

But there was life, life that, before her disbelieving and horrified eyes, began to move, squirming and writhing with purpose, jostling back and forth in near silent malevolence.

"Oh my God," Tiffany whispered. She didn't hear her own words however; they were lost in the insanity of what she was seeing.

Legs began to emerge from the blackness, hairy legs that as they found purchase on the edge of the window frame, hoisted the bulbous forms they were attached to out into the room.

The spiders clung to the wall. Dozens of the beasts scampered every which way, quickly covering half the room with her hateful eyes and hungry maws.

Tiffany's arms dropped to her sides. She was defeated, and resigned herself to her grisly fate. The spiders had transformed everything into more spiders, including the entire room, the house, and perhaps even the world outside. Everything had been changed into things that bite.

The floor began to shift. It undulated slightly at first, and then with more force, gradually swelling into smooth rhythmic motions.

Tiffany stared as legs, eyes, and fangs lifted from what used to be dust-coated floorboards and tattered carpets, and within the span of a minute were awash with movement.

It's not a house at all. Everything is made of...them. Everything.

Her hand started to swell. She felt feverish.

It's the venom.

Her waist began to shrink, effectively bisecting her body into two distinct sections: abdomen and thorax.

It's changing me!

Bright orange hair sprouted from her pores, covering every inch of her wracked body. Four limbs poked out from her sides. Starting out as hairy knobs, they quickly extended to the length of her arms and legs and developed additional joints that cracked and popped when she flexed them.

I'm becoming something else...

Blue-tinged hair grew on her many limbs at even dispersals, clashing beautifully with the orange coloring of the surrounding hair.

something not human.

Her head flattened, molding itself into the top of the thorax. Three pairs of glossy black eyes rose through the mass of hair, joining the pair of existing eyes, which had changed to match their neighbors. And a set of chelicera with razor-sharp fangs protruding from them, and each connected to a pulsating venom sac, dangled over the mouth, itself now a tube-like structure that bore no resemblance to the human orifice it had once been.

Something...something else.

The spider, larger than any others around it, the size of a human, crouched down on the bristling floor of the house. It clicked its oversized fangs in anticipation of sinking them

into prey. It wanted nothing more, like its deadly brethren, than to create more like itself. Any traces of its former existence had vanished; any residual links to its past, erased. It was a different species now, one wholly intent on world domination.

Tiffany reared back, and with lightning speed, scuttled out of the window and into her destiny.

Spiders

As I sit on my musty couch with a half-empty drink in my hand, I see a spider scurry across the room.

Normally, I'd jump out of my skin. I'm terrified of those creepy little eight-legged things. Have been ever since I was a kid. I saw one (a dirty-yellow thing the size of a nickel) crawl onto my plate of food, and from then on they frightened me. I was only about eight or nine years old at the time so you could imagine how traumatized I was.

And to think that I almost ate it!

But the reason the spider in my living room doesn't startle me is simple:

I *know* it.

Yes, I know it well. I've seen it before. I recognize it.

Most people would think I'm crazy. They'd say I've lost my mind, lost my touch with reality, flipped my lid.

I suppose in a way, they'd be right.

But then again, maybe not.

The spider suddenly stops. It gracefully turns around and faces me. Leaning up on its pencil-thin back legs, it flashes half-inch long fangs in my direction. I can see drops of milky-white venom trickle from the tips.

I have this instinctive feeling that it knows me as well. It recognizes me, as I do it.

After a few seconds of displaying its weapons, the spider returns to its normal stance and scuttles into my bedroom.

I shudder at the implications.

As I look at my cell phone encased in thick blanket of silk, I can only smile. *They're very thorough*, I muse to myself.

I glance at the front door. It's covered in a sheet of web so dense I can hardly see it. Several dozen spiders of varying size ramble through the silky mess, obviously to make sure I can't escape.

"Richard, come to me now."

I toss my beer to the floor and stand up. I can't control my legs, but it doesn't matter. I would heed her call regardless.

I obey and stumble into the bedroom. A small spider doesn't get out of the way in time and is crushed beneath my foot. I grimace as I feel its gooey innards squeeze up between my toes.

"I'm sorry," I mumble as my heart tears. I hardly knew the bug, but it still hurts.

"Richard, come to me now!"

I obey the command from my wife and stumble into the bedroom.

She is on our bed. A cushion of silk supports all eight of her legs, as well as her heavy abdomen. Her fangs curve inward toward her delicate but deadly mouth. Fine hairs bristle across her body.

I try not to look at the hundreds of spiders that are scrambling around the room. They vary in size from no bigger than a fingernail up to two feet across.

I catch a glimpse of one (my first) that's as big as a fully grown dog. It glares at me from just inside the closet door.

"Richard," my wife whispers through her fangs. "Come to me now."

I make my way over to our bed, and climb in next to her.

My wife immediately sinks her fangs into my neck. I feel the potent venom course through my veins, as I have so many times before. I know it's what she uses to control me, to coax from me what she wants (more children), but I don't care. I also know that she needs love.

"I love you," I moan.

"And I love you," she hisses, and then envelopes me in her grasp.

Andy's lamp

The lamp had moved. Andy was sure of it. The soft yellow glow from the 60-watt bulb had shifted slightly, causing vague shadows in the room to move as if alive. Granted it wasn't much movement, but it was there. There was no doubt about it.

Andy forced himself to relax, settling back into his worn recliner with his small caliber semi-automatic handgun resting in his lap. It was an older model, a gift from his senile grandfather, but it still worked effectively. The silencer he bought for it had proved to be money well spent. Silence was a necessity in his situation. He couldn't afford to let any of his neighbors hear anything out of the ordinary, such as a gun firing.

He focused on the lamp again, studying it closely, waiting for it to move again. It wore its pale yellow shade like a hat. Fondling the trigger of the gun he swore to himself that he would take action this time if anything moved. This time he wouldn't hesitate. This time he would be ready.

Several minutes elapsed. The monotonous ticking of the wall clock was the only sound in the house, echoing in the room. Andy was fighting sleep, his weary mind drifting in and out of consciousness. He knew very well that falling asleep could be a big mistake, but still found himself dozing off. The last time he did the spider thing came, slithering out of the refrigerator, week old milk and cheese dripping from its bloated body. He had woken up just in time to flatten it with a few sharp swings from his trusty baseball bat, Woody.

Eventually he had abandoned his bat in favor of a more versatile and efficient weapon, his gun. In a strange way he actually was anxious for the spider thing to appear again. Surely bullets would do a far more effective job of dispatching it than good old Woody.

His troubled mind wandered back to the first time the spider thing had appeared. He had just come home from work, back when he had a job, and promptly fastened himself to his chair in front of the television set. He was tired and suffering from a cold and all he wanted to do was flip through channels, a routine that he found himself slipping into more and more frequently. As the newscast lady read about the day's events her pretty face started to distort. Her light blue eyes slid apart further and further until they were next to her ears. And from the vacant spaces where they had been emerged the glowing evil of the spider thing, its thick skull splitting open the lady's head as it snaked its way into the light of the news station room.

Next came the legs, which sprouted from the sides of the TV and immediately began to thrash up and down as if throwing a fit. The appendages were thin, almost skeletal, and were covered in glistening slime.

The newscast lady continued on about a horrible car accident that morning on Interstate 696, completely oblivious to the swollen abdomen rising directly behind her head. She was pretty still, although in a horror movie type of way now, and Andy found himself wondering if he was hallucinating.

But he wasn't.

The spider thing's razor sharp fangs clicked together methodically, dripping a foul greenish substance that Andy guessed was some type of venom. It focused its multiple eyes on Andy then, and he before he knew what he was doing he ran to his bedroom and grabbed old Woody and ended the nightmare, and his TV, with three quick swings.

There it was again! The lamp had moved! Andy raised his gun slightly, leveling it at the inanimate object as he pondered whether or not to finally take action. The lamp stood motionless on the end table, illuminating the room with its yellowed light. It almost dared him to fire at it. He watched it methodically, still undecided if he should blow the thing apart before it changed, before the spider thing came. Too many times in the past he had waited too long.

One time the spider thing nearly got to him, grazing its jagged teeth along his forearm, leaving a four-inch scar and undeniable proof of its existence. Since then if he ever doubted that it was all real all he needed to do was to look at his arm.

The lamp started to jiggle, a little at first, but then much more pronounced. It jerked forward, then backwards. Its lampshade shifted to one side. The light bulb shattered. The cord slipped out of the wall socket and swung high into the air before crashing down to the floor. Andy watched in horror as the glistening legs slid out from the sides of the lamp. For all the mental preparation he had done he still found himself shaking considerably, so much so that he had trouble steadying his gun on the creature.

The face of the spider thing emerged from the lamp and focused on Andy, hissing at him so loudly that a small mirror on a nearby wall cracked. Andy stared into the dull, emotionless eyes of the thing. He saw his distorted reflection in its eyes. He saw his death.

Gathering what strength he could Andy leveled his gun at the thing's head. He squeezed the trigger four times in quick succession, each rattling his already frail nerves. And after the smoke cleared he leaned forward to view his handiwork.

All he saw was a shattered lamp. Sharp pieces of it lay strewn all across the table and floor and four bullet holes decorated the wall. Andy grunted in disgust. The mess was terrible and would require a lot of cleanup.

How could he have missed it? Where was its body? And why no blood?

There was however another explanation.

Perhaps it was all in his mind. Hallucinations. Stress. Imagination. Maybe he had just imagined the whole thing.

But what about the wound on his arm? Surely that was proof the thing existed.

But then he remembered the accident he had when he was fixing his truck. A sudden slip with a large screwdriver and bingo…a huge, bloody gash. Just like the one on his arm.

Feeling relieved for the first time in days Andy suddenly realized he was hungry. Sauntering into the kitchen he made himself a quick sandwich. Disturbing thoughts interrupted his meal though, such as where the thing had come from in the first place or what it really wanted. But there was nothing he could do about it now. One way or another it was gone.

He finished his meal and fell back into his recliner half asleep. For the first time in ages he was able to completely relax, finally not having to worry about being attacked by alien spider monsters. He would work on bettering himself. First thing in the morning he would scan the want ads for any available job he could lay his hands on. And then he would ask the cute girl across the street out on a date. And then he would look for a nicer car.

He found himself periodically looking over at the remains of his lamp, just to make sure there wasn't anything attempting to crawl out of it, but saw nothing except for splintered pieces of it lying on the floor.

Eventually he started to doze off. The day had been a long one and he was very tired. So tired that he didn't notice the thin legs sliding out from one of the shattered pieces of the lamp.

A Spider in the Window

Wyatt groaned as he pulled out the vacuum cleaner from the closet.

"And don't forget the den," his mother nagged. "There's more of Mr. Furry's hair in there."

Wyatt nodded, knowing very well that his mother couldn't see him.

"Wyatt? Did you hear me?"

"Yes, Mom."

Plugging the vacuum cleaner into a nearby wall outlet, Wyatt started his chores.

He finished the front room quickly, noting that there wasn't much fur, but as he progressed to the hallway, and then the guest bedroom, he was shocked at just how much of the stuff there was.

Dozens of tiny hairballs littered the carpet. Each was a part of his cat's fur coat, that for reasons unknown to him, apparently came loose from his pet and wadded up into the little fuzzy landmines he now had to clean up.

Morning sunlight streamed through the blinds in the den, embellishing the hairballs on the futon and carpet.

Wyatt glanced at the window. A sinewy cobweb gleamed in the light. It was fastened directly over a small hole in the screen, as if sealing it off.

His eyes roamed for any sign of the spider that had built it, but he couldn't see one.

His mind shifted to the job he had to do. With a groan, he turned the vacuum cleaner on and began to push it across the floor.

Mr. Furry strolled into the room, bringing with him a new collection of fuzzy hairballs. Several floated from his body and settled on the carpet.

Wyatt switched off the vacuum and stared at his pet. He felt his irritation grow, but it faded just as quickly when he noticed the bald spots.

"Mr. Furry? What's the matter, boy?"

The cat tilted its head slightly as if in answer to his questions and then turned and gracefully walked out of the room.

And then Wyatt noticed something else:

one of the hairballs moved!

"Must be my imagination," he reasoned with himself. "Now I'm seeing things."

Another clump of fur, this one the size of a golf ball, slowly began to roll across the carpet. It grew with every inch it covered, picking up more stray fur as it went.

Wyatt froze. The vacuum cleaner cord dangled in his hand. Mr. Furry's gentle meow echoed from the next room.

The hairball reached the far wall of the room. It had grown to the size of a baseball and continued to bump against the drywall as if it were trying to push its way through it.

Wyatt could only stare at it.

Then he saw other movement in the room, and in the hallway, and in the window. Balls of cat's fur, some as large as a man's fist, rolled back and forth. Most glistened with moisture, leaving sickly, hair-laden trails in their wake.

One nudged up against Wyatt's foot. He stepped back, and was startled when thin, gray hairs stretched out from the central mass and reached eagerly for him. A milky fluid dribbled from the tips of the hairs.

"Mom!" Wyatt cried. "Mom! Where are you?"

But his cries went unanswered.

A foreboding chill swept through him. He was trapped and he knew it. God only knew where his mother was, and the balls of fur were multiplying at an alarming rate. Where once there were only a few, now there were dozens. They formed right before his eyes from the carpet and futon and blocked the doorway.

And still more were rolling in from the hallway.

Wyatt knew his only chance was the vacuum cleaner. He could use it like a weapon, maybe sling it around the room, batting the little beasts as if they were baseballs.

But one look at the dust container on the machine, and he knew it was a bad idea.

The cylinder was bustling with fur.

Fur that was *alive*.

Wyatt threw the vacuum to the ground, which also proved to be a bad idea because the impact cracked the plastic reservoir and released more of the things into the room.

In a flash, there were hundreds of the lethal hairballs tumbling all around. They shot out long thin feelers that groped for purchase.

They surrounded Wyatt. Feelers snapped at his feet. They began to roll up his legs, ignoring his vain attempts at swatting them away. In seconds, he was covered in a swarming blanket of carnivorous fur.

The last thing he saw was a fleeting glimpse of the window. The cobweb in the corner swayed from the chaos, but remained intact.

*   *   *   *

Mr. Furry poked his head into the room. He felt a chill, a result of having no fur left on his body, and was nervous because of all the commotion in the house.

His green eyes focused on the massive lump of fur in the center of the room. It moved, but only slightly, just enough to give it an appearance of life. If he were smarter, he would have understood that the fur he was seeing was *his* fur. But, lacking the intelligence to grasp what had happened, he merely continued on his way.

And in the den's window, camouflaged by its web, squatted a creature that resembled a wolf spider. It observed the carnage in the room, and satisfied, crawled through the hole in the screen and out into the beautiful morning. It had found the perfect catalyst for its young (the cat's fur), and now all it had to do was wait for the multiplying process to begin. Soon, its spawn would spread to all corners of the world to find suitable hosts for their own young, and so on, and so on, until the planet was overrun.

Then it would move on to the next world.

Puppy-Sized

Cassie switched off the vacuum cleaner and took a deep breath. She stood at the entrance to the living room, the very room she hated going into.

It was a nice part of the house, a cozy, warm room that was lined with built-in mahogany bookshelves and attractive silk window dressings. A plasma TV hung above a spacious fireplace, and an ornate oak desk, custom-made and inlaid with silver trim, stood before a large bay window. It was cluttered with her husband Frank's various papers and an expensive computer monitor. A small brass lamp stood at attention on a corner of the desk

Cassie could see Frank sitting there, a cigarette in one hand and a gold-plated pen in the other.

Her attention swung over to a large glass aquarium. It was perched on a steel-frame stand and gleamed in the sunlight that streamed into the room. It stretched eight feet long and two feet tall, and the lid, a heavy-duty iron grate, was slightly ajar near one end.

She stepped into the room, closed the door behind her, and walked up to the aquarium. Fear battled with her curiosity over control of her body, but the former won out.

She secured the lid back in place, and peered into the tank. A thick mat of peat moss carpeted the floor of the aquarium. A massive hollowed out decorative log big enough to house a small dog occupied one side of the tank, a faded ceramic bowl with stagnant water the other.

Cassie felt revulsion seep into her gut. She didn't like spiders (especially big ones), and judging by the size of the aquarium (as well as the log) the one hiding was a big one.

Too big as far as she was concerned.

And Frank loved spiders.

Cassie straightened up and realized that she had been standing too close to the tank. Her body trembled as her head began the process of plaguing her with a migraine.

She stepped away from the aquarium, and was about to bolt out of the room when she noticed a glimpse of movement on the far side of the log. It was small (no more than a slight jostling of the substrate), but it was there nevertheless.

With bated breath she stared at the spot and waited for something to emerge from the peat moss.

Seconds ticked by, gradually sliding into minutes.

Cassie forced herself to look away.

Maybe I imagined it.

And then, almost as if responding to her thoughts, something moved again.

She did a double take and waited.

A tiny nub of something flesh-colored poked up through the substrate. It was small, but as more of it emerged, it began to take on a definite and recognizable form.

A finger. It was a finger. A human digit bleached from lack of blood flow and stiffened by the merciless onset of rigor mortis.

Cassie froze where she stood. She struggled to regain control of her body, but fear held her tight in its grip.

"Oh…my…God," she mumbled through clenched teeth.

As she watched, the finger rose from the ground cover. Soon it was flanked by other fingers, similar in size and stage of decomposition. Each was stiff and bloodless.

Something shiny caught her attention.

It was a ring on one of the fingers. And not just any ring, a ring Cassie recognized. She could see the custom-made diamond that Frank had put on it when they were first married.

"Frank?"

The fingers twisted upward until the remainder of the hand they were attached to rose into view. Clots of substrate clung to the dead flesh, adding to the ghastly appearance of the hand.

As Cassie watched, more lifted up out of the ground cover, and in the span of half a minute, the entire arm up to the elbow was exposed.

There was no doubt about it. It was Frank's arm.

With her heart in her throat, Cassie stepped back from the aquarium. Her mind raced in a thousand different directions. She knew she should call the police, but the anguish over losing her husband paralyzed her body. She stood in the center of the room, not knowing what to do.

A thought struck her like a freight train.

What killed him?

She rushed over to Frank's desk and snatched the phone off its base. She punched in 9-1-1 and waited for a dispatcher.

Nothing. The line was dead.

"Hello? Hello?" she cried into the receiver, even though she knew there was no one on the line.

She slammed the phone back on the base and gripped the cord in her sweaty hand. She followed it down off the desk, nearly falling over when the neatly snipped line drew up into her fingers.

"This can't be happening."

Something occurred to her then. It was the only explanation for how Frank wound up in the aquarium.

The spider. The God-awful beast that had to be hiding in the hollowed out log.

Cassie turned and faced the aquarium. She wanted to leave, to just run out of the room and get help, but something made her stay. She *needed* to know what happened to her husband, even at her own risk.

The hand was still there, jutting up from the substrate like some crazy Halloween decoration, and with a sick feeling in her stomach, she looked at the log.

The opening was nearly a foot and a half wide and pitch dark inside. Nothing stirred in the blackness. A few random crickets scurried around the entrance to the miniature black hole, but seemed to sense danger and avoided venturing inside.

Cassie strained to see inside the log. She couldn't imagine a spider big enough to need such a large hiding spot. She'd never seen the beast, only the tank, but just the thought made her shudder.

The arm moved again, although not by its own volition. The fingers were frozen with rigor mortis, but the arm rose up, as something beneath it was gently pushing it upward.

Cassie backed away from the horrid display. She grabbed a letter opener on the desk and wielded it as if it were a dagger. Somehow she knew she would have to defend herself.

A great explosion erupted in the aquarium. Tufts of substrate shot into the air as the arm, and the body it was attached to, were pushed up for all to see. Clumps of clotted blood and flecks of decayed flesh dotted the limb. Chalk-white bone protruded out from beneath the skin, and a terrible stench permeated the grisly relic.

It seemed as if the arm was pointing at her.

Cassie fought the urge to vomit. The letter opener in her hand felt as useless as the phone had been.

The substrate began to move. Where the arm ended, a clump of ground cover lifted and fell in smooth rhythms before something else made its presence known.

And it wasn't part of Frank.

A leg, bristling with dense black hair and droplets of dried blood, lifted up. It was multi-segmented and moved with an air of confident stillness.

~ 66 ~

Cassie watched as the horrible appendage slowly rose, inch by inch, until it revealed what it was attached to.

A bulbous and grainy-black abdomen emerged, and with an equally grotesque and slightly smaller head in front of it. Four sets of glossy black eyes glared out from their recessed sockets. A pair of glistening fangs hung in the air below its head.

Cassie recoiled from the sight. The spider was enormous, the size of a puppy, perhaps bigger, and sported an evil visage that animals simply should not possess.

And the worst part of it was was what dangled in its mouth, hanging down between its 3-inch fags like some piece of ghoulish jewelry.

It was a human head, stripped of most of its flesh and barely recognizable as Frank. The eyes, clouded over and staring at nothing, only added to the horrific display.

The spider let the head fall. It made no sound as it crashed to the mat of substrate and rolled to its side. A dull-gray tongue lolled out of the mouth.

Cassie screamed. Her voice seemed to be a separate entity, a different part of her body altogether, wholly able to express itself individually.

"Help! Somebody help me!"

The spider tilted its head to the side as if puzzled by its intended prey's reaction to its presence.

But it made no difference. It was hungry and wasn't about to let a meal get away.

The spider crept forward with perfectly synchronized movements toward the front of the tank. Its many eyes focused on Cassie. Hunger throbbed in its brain. Its fangs clicked in anticipation. It was a predator, streamlined to maximum efficiency and intent on obtaining sustenance. Nothing would stop it. Nothing ever had.

It swung one of its front legs against the tank, shattering the reinforced glass with ease, and in the blink of an eye, darted out into the room toward its next meal.

The Manipulators

The house loomed before the boys like a Gothic statue over cowering worshipers. The orange glow from the sun setting on the horizon only scarcely lit the towering structure, giving it an aura of gloom and potentially dangerous mystery. A gentle breeze, almost too light to be noticeable, flitted through the sparse, mostly dead vegetation.

"I'm not going in there," Brad announced. Being the oldest member of the group his word was usually followed by the three younger boys.

Terry, a usually shy kid who had tagged along at the last minute, did a double take. "What?" he said with raised eyebrows. "You, the toughest person I know doesn't want to see if the treasure really exists?"

There was a tinge of disdain in his voice. It was no secret that he was vying for the position of leader in the group, a fact that Brad was all too aware of.

Brad straightened up and regained his composure. A small flashlight dangled from his hand.

He eyed his clan. Not wanting to appear weak, he took a few deep breaths and reasserted his authority over his subjects.

"Of course not!" he said with as straight a face as he could muster. "I'm not scared of any old house." He strutted along the walkway, onto the porch, and up to the front door. "Come on, guys, let's see where that treasure is at."

The two youngest boys (brothers Alex and Jimmy) stood on the edge of the property. They were scared, and wanted to go home, but even at their young age the allure of treasure was hard to resist.

"Why would somebody hide treasure in an old house?" Jimmy asked. His arms twitched nervously at his sides.

"Because," Brad said from the front porch. "They knew nobody would look there. It's the perfect spot to hide something."

"Yeah," Terry added. "I heard that they robbed Kent Bank over on Mason and Potter in downtown and stashed the loot, including a bunch of gold bars, in this house."

"That's right," Brad chimed in, "And up until now nobody's taken it seriously enough to investigate. Then they disappeared. Nobody saw them ever again."

Alex said nothing. He stood next to his brother in silence, fear and doubt etched across his pale face.

A knot formed in his gut when he caught a glimpse of movement in one of the upstairs windows. Somebody (or something) gently parted the tattered drapes, kept them open for a few seconds, and then closed them again. A wispy shadow remained behind the thin, dirty fabric.

It appeared to have more than two arms.

"Alex, what's the matter?" Jimmy asked his brother. "You look like you've seen a ghost."

"Maybe I did," Alex replied through clenched teeth. He pointed at the window. "Up there, behind the curtain."

Terry stopped on the walkway and followed Alex's gesture.

He also saw something in the window.

"What's holding you guys up?" Brad called back. He was jostling with the front door, trying to see if it would open for him.

Terry suddenly felt a paralyzing chill sweep over him. A phobia he had dredged itself up from the very depths of his mind and presented itself, with all the potential scenarios his imagination could attach to it, to him for consideration.

He was scared of spiders.

It was irrational; he never had a bad experience with the little creepy crawlies, but he still harbored a debilitating fear of them. It was as much a part of him as his love for his mother or enjoying swimming on a hot summer day.

"Come on, guys," Brad said again, this time with a substantial amount of impatience in his voice. His subjects were misbehaving and he didn't like it. "I've just about got the door open." He jiggled the rusty door knob in his hands to emphasize his point.

Alex and Jimmy didn't move from their spot. Both were entertaining frightening memories they had with spiders.

Jimmy had found a hidden path while on a camping trip that led to a moss-strewn depression in the ground. He didn't notice the light layer of cobweb that lined the hole, nor the creature that had claimed it for its home.

He stumbled as he leaned over the depression, having seen something glint in the light, and quickly found himself face-to-face with a hairy nightmare the size of a baseball.

The spider snapped at him with its generously-abundant fangs.

He narrowly managed to avoid being bitten.

Nobody believed him about how big the spider had been.

Alex had his unfortunate introduction to the world of spiders when he sat in class one day and felt a sharp pain in his calf. He immediately reached down to investigate, and after pulling up his pant leg, was horrified to see a rather large wolf spider, writhing babies still clinging to their mother's back, scuttle out from its unwarranted sanctuary and run across the room at lightning speed.

It vanished behind a bookshelf, leaving more than a few of its offspring, dead from the trauma of its hasty escape, in its wake.

Alex was scarred for life, on his leg as well as his psyche, and from then on avoided anything that walked on eight legs.

"Come on, guys," Brad said from the front porch. He had managed to dislodge the doorknob from its flimsy seat in the door and nudge the barrier open. "Man, you guys are such wimps, totally gutless. If I find that treasure, I am going to…"

The words died in his throat when a pitch-black void revealed itself inside the doorway.

Terry turned back around and saw Brad standing at the threshold to the house. He wasn't going inside. In fact, he wasn't moving at all.

Brad was terrified. The darkness could be concealing so many things, things possibly dangerous, perhaps even deadly. Things like a psychotic killer just waiting for his next victim to stumble into his grasp. Or a wild animal that had found refuge in the building and was growing hungrier by the minute. Or maybe even a visitor from another planet, an extraterrestrial who was sent as a scout to determine the strength of the enemy before relaying the information in preparation for the invasion.

Brad had to stop himself. He was letting his imagination run wild. He'd been watching too many horror movies lately, reading too many scary books, staying up too late at night.

But there was one thing he wasn't imagining: just how dark it was inside the house. And since it was so dark, his greatest fear could be concealed by the darkness, a fear that no matter how much he lied to himself or tried his best to look tough in front of others, still dwelled deep within his very soul.

Spiders.

He tried to affix an incident in his past that would at least help explain his irrational phobia, but couldn't. Sure, he'd had brushes with all manners of animals throughout his childhood like any other kid, but nothing noteworthy.

He could only sum it up as the way a spider moved: its eight legs gracefully synchronized with each other; its abdomen and thorax gently undulating with each step it took; its fangs tasting the air in anticipation of embedding themselves in some juicy prey. All these aspects, coupled with its ability to move at breakneck speed or flashing its black eyes at any creature in its way, gave the spider unparalleled access to anyone's deepest dreams.

Brad looked at the sheet of blackness before him. Nothing stirred in it. It was just a yawning chasm, void of life or warmth, inviting and yet distant.

He took a deep breath, clicked on his flashlight, and stepped into the house.

I can't let the guys think I'm scared. I can't.

Terry, Alex, and Jimmy all watched Brad, their illustrious self-appointed leader, disappear into the darkness.

None of them spoke. The three boys only stared at the house. The front door was still open, the same spot where Brad had stepped through into its mysteries.

And now he was gone.

"Brad?" Terry called out. "Where are you?" He remembered what he'd seen in the window, and try as he might, couldn't shake the image from his mind.

"Where'd he go?" Jimmy and Alex asked in unison.

Terry ignored the brother's question, only motioning for them to follow him up to the house. "Come on, guys," he said with as much courage as he could muster. "We got to see what's inside this place once and for all."

"But why?" Jimmy asked. His brother was already walking toward Terry, but he remained still. "I don't want to go in there."

"Because," Terry countered. "If we don't, we'll never know, and that will stick with you for the rest of your life."

Even at his young age, Jimmy understood that what Terry said was true. He'd go crazy wondering what was in the house. Spiders or no spiders, he'd heard once that the best way to conquer your fears is to face them. So if there were some terrible things crawling around inside the house and he confronted them he'd see that they weren't so bad after all. He'd see that they were more scared of him than he was of them.

"All right," he mumbled, joining Terry and his brother on the porch.

The front door was still open, but there was no sign of Brad. Only a black wall stood before the boys. It revealed nothing. Not even the scarce and rapidly-dwindling daylight penetrated the gloom.

"Brad? Where are you?" Terry asked.

No answer.

Terry leaned into the doorway, being ever so careful not to touch the darkness. He didn't know why but he didn't want to touch it.

"Brad? Answer me."

Still no reply.

Feeling a sense of courage, as well as urgency, Terry clenched his hands into fists and stepped into the house.

Instantly, he felt cold envelope his body. The air was dank, slightly tainted with decay and just a hint of something sour. It reminded him of when his father would dump out used motor oil from his truck.

"Brad?"

He clicked his flashlight on and roamed the darkness with the overmatched beam of light. It only penetrated a few feet, revealing barren, dry-rotted walls and a threadbare carpet runner.

"Brad? Where are you?"

Jimmy and Alex came up behind him, so close, they nearly bumped into him.

"Where is he?" Jimmy asked.

"I don't know," Terry replied. He had a bad feeling about Brad, a feeling that not only was something wrong, but very wrong."

"He's probably just playing a joke on us," Alex said. "You know, trying to act tough and show he's not scared."

"Either that or he's found the treasure and wants to keep it all for himself," Jimmy added in an annoyed tone.

Terry took another step forward. He felt every single heartbeat in his chest, every blinking of his eyes, every churn in his stomach.

Something scuttled over his foot, causing him to jump back. He hit the frame of the door with his back. He had to force himself to keep from crying out.

"What's the matter?" Jimmy asked.

Terry regained his composure. "Nothing," he lied. "Nothing at all."

If the brothers became too scared they'd refuse to go into the house, and that was somewhere he didn't want to go alone.

"There you guys are," Brad said. His voice rang through the darkness. "What took you so long?"

Terry immediately swung his flashlight up in the direction of the voice. The yellow beam landed squarely on the grinning but annoyed face of Brad.

"Hey, cut that out," he said while trying to block the glare with his hands. "What's the big idea?"

Jimmy and Alex were hunched up behind Terry.

"Where's your flashlight?" Jimmy asked.

Brad shrugged. "I must've lost it. Anyway, come on in. I think I found the treasure." He gestured behind him. "It's down in the cellar, at the end of this hallway. Follow me." He turned and strutted into the darkness, quickly vanishing down the corridor.

The three boys didn't move. The prospect of finding the treasure filled their thoughts, but was neighbors with the possibility of danger. Something wasn't right, and the feeling was mutual between each one of them.

"Well? What are we going to do?" Jimmy asked. He was nervous, and it rang in his voice.

Terry thought for a moment and then said: "What choice do we have? We can't just leave him in there. And besides, maybe he did find something."

Alex and Jimmy grew smiles. The thought of treasure, free for the taking, enticed them to venture into the house. Their fears were still there, but realistically they knew there was nothing to worry about. Spiders, with the exception of a few species of tarantula, the redback and black widows, the Brazilian wanderer, and the infamous funnel web spiders of Australia, were generally harmless to man, causing not much more than a pinprick with their fangs that wasn't any worse than a bee sting.

The brothers cautiously followed Terry into the house. Each held a small flashlight in a shaky hand, and mentally noted how the darkness seemed to swallow the light with ease.

"Where do you think he went?" Jimmy asked. More than once he thought he felt something crawl across his feet, but dismissed it as his imagination. He surprised himself with the courage he was showing. He hoped some of it would rub off on his brother.

Alex however, wasn't feeling courageous. He was scared. He was terrified. He was having trouble staying on his feet.

The beam from his flashlight swept across the wall to his left, giving a brief and frightening glimpse of a large spider with a leg span of six to seven inches. It clung to the wall with its head facing down toward the floor.

It quickly crawled out of sight.

Alex stopped dead in his tracks. "Guys, I saw spider, a big one too. It was on the wall."

Terry and Jimmy turned around, their flashlights trained on Alex. They could see the fear on his face.

"Where?" Jimmy asked, not really wanting an answer.

"There."

Alex pointed to the spot where the spider had been, but when the light shone on it, there was no sign of the beast.

"It was there, I swear it was."

"We believe you," Jimmy said. He put a hand on his brother's shoulder.

"Are you guys coming, or what?"

Brad suddenly appeared at the end of the hallway. He was bathed, ever so slightly, in the faded glow of the flashlight that dangled from his hand.

"Brad!" Terry cried. "Where'd you go?"

Brad ignored the question, instead motioning for the others to follow him into the darkness. "Come on, guys," he said. "Follow me. I'll show you what I found."

Jimmy grew excited. "Is it the treasure? Did you find the treasure?"

Alex however, had his thoughts on the spider he'd seen. He wasn't really that interested in anything (treasure included) if it involved venturing into the house any more than he already was.

Terry was hesitant to follow Brad, and not because of spiders, but because of how Brad looked. He seemed normal for the most part, but the way he moved, almost like he was being directed, controlled somehow.

"Follow me. I found the treasure. There's gold and stacks of money. It's really old, but it's still money. Come on, guys, we're gonna be rich."

And then Terry saw it.

He rubbed his eyes to make sure he wasn't imagining it.

Strings. There were nearly a dozen strings above Brad. Nearly a dozen that trailed down in straight taut lines from some shadow-obscured source, and were attached to Brad's body: one on each shoulder, one behind the neck, one to the head, and several more at varying spots such as the arms and upper back.

They pulled him along like some bizarre human marionette.

"Follow me, guys. I found the treasure."

Terry watched the spectacle with a sense of detached terror and fascination.

"Brad, we need to get out of this place now! We have to leave, and fast!"

Something moved in the shadows above Brad. It wasn't something big, but instead seemed to be comprised of many smaller things, like a swarm.

Terry knew he would regret it but he raised his flashlight above the still figure of his friend.

Spiders. Literally hundreds of the beasts squirmed in every direction imaginable. Fangs scraped against abdomens, and legs brushed against heads and eyes. Innumerable legs fought for position.

The creatures hissed when the light shone on them, filling the hallway with an otherworldly song of danger.

And through it all Brad remained oblivious to the horrible mess above his head. His expression remained unchanged.

"Come on, guys. Follow me. I found the treasure."

Alex and Jimmy couldn't speak. They simply stared, open-mouthed, at the creatures of their nightmares, the things that crawled up and down their spines whenever they felt afraid.

Terry forced himself to pull his flashlight away from the spiders. He had already seen too much. He'd already remember far more than he would ever be able to endure.

The light trailed down Brad's body, and eventually settled on his feet, which hung a few inches above the floor. They dangled there like flies caught in a web, waiting and lifeless.

"Come on, guys. I found the treasure."

The spiders increased their frantic movements. Dozens of the larger ones worked threads of web this way and that, causing Brad to move accordingly. A thread, skull-white in the yellow beam of the flashlight, was jerked backward by one of the spiders, causing Brad's head to move with it, fully exposing his eerily-normal face.

"Treasure. There's lots of treasure."

And then, so suddenly it didn't seem possible, Brad was yanked down the hallway and into an adjoining room, leaving a dozen spiders still clinging to the strands of webbing that were attached to him. They hung in the air like trapeze artists, gracefully holding on to the threads with ease, suspended in the dark, dank corridor.

"We need to go now," Alex mumbled in a terrified trance. He began to step back the way they had come.

"Yeah," Jimmy agreed. He moved in cautious unison with his brother.

But when the boys felt something under their feet, something soft and yielding, something organic, something that squealed in pain when stepped on, they froze where they stood, too afraid to move, too afraid to breathe.

The spiders scurried across their feet and into the darkness.

Terry had seen enough, but instead of giving in to his fears, he pushed forward. He was determined to see this through. Spiders, although creepy, couldn't hurt him. He was a strong young man. He was smart. He was agile.

He stepped down the hallway, ever mindful of the clattering masses around him, until he stood at the archway were Brad had vanished.

A ten-inch spider scrambled up to his feet, gazed at him with expressionless black eyes, and crawled away.

Terry didn't look behind him, instead focusing on the light from his flashlight.

Brad stood in the center of the room. He was obviously dead (his abdomen was split open down the middle and seethed with spiders), and was wrapped from head to toe (except for his abdomen) in a dense sheet of webbing. His ghostlike face peered out through the covering in a frozen expression of pain and fear.

Terry knew he had been dead in the hallway as well. His body was filled with spiders. They were manipulating him. How or for what purpose he didn't know, but that didn't matter. What did matter was getting out of the house alive.

Alex and Jimmy had reached the front door. They did their best to ignore the spiders around them: hanging from the ceiling; scurrying around the floor; crawling up and down the walls; darting in and out of the shadows, but were having trouble doing so. Their arachnophobia was being thrust in their faces, making it nearly impossible to resist.

Jimmy reached for the door handle. He missed it on the first try but found it on the next. He twisted it savagely, his desperation to escape overruling any sense of caution or hesitancy he still had.

The door wouldn't open. It moved a quarter of an inch, perhaps slightly more, but was jammed.

Jimmy pulled on it with all his strength, but still nothing.

"It won't open," he said. His flashlight fell from his hand and crashed to the floor, breaking on contact.

Alex reached for the door handle. He held his flashlight in his other hand, but the batteries were dying. The light was fading fast.

A small spider, no larger than a quarter, leaped down from above and landed on his hand. In a flash, it punctured his skin with its sharp fangs, eliciting a cry of pain from Alex.

Two dots of blood welled up on the flesh.

"It bit me! It bit me!"

He shook it off, dropping his flashlight in the process. It also broke on the floor.

The hallway was plunged into near darkness. The only light came from Terry's flashlight, and he was shining into the room where Brad was.

Terry turned and aimed his light at the brothers. They were huddled together in front of the door.

Alex was cradling one of his arms.

The door behind them was sealed shut. A thick mat of webbing covered where it met the frame, effectively creating a solid structure which through no light could be seen. The only area that was untouched by the web was the doorknob.

"Come on, guys," Brad's voice echoed down the hallway. "Follow me."

Terry swung back around and trained his light on Brad. Spiders swarmed around his body, and his feet still dangled above the floor. The light reflected off the web strands that held him up.

Something touched the back of Terry's head, just below the hairline.

He whirled around and swatted at it.

He looked at his hand and was hardly surprised to see two dots of blood and a single thread of silk that trailed upward. It was as thick as a man's finger and so dense it appeared solid.

And then he felt something touch each of his shoulders. Panic overtook him and he frantically began dancing around in a mad effort to remove the webbing.

But he couldn't get it off. The thread stuck fast to his body.

More strands of webbing drifted down and fastened to him. They attached to his head, his arms, his back.

Terry cried out in horror as his entire body was lifted off the ground and pulled into the room. He could feel the painful jerks of the webbing, but was powerless to stop it. His arms and legs were useless to him now, mere extensions of his body that served no purpose other than being used to move him around.

Spiders of all shapes and sizes immediately slid down the threads and began to crawl over Terry, sending his panic and fear into entirely new realms. He tried to call for help, could only mutter incoherent ramblings. He felt numerous bites and burning pain coursing through his body, and sensed an unusual and frightening change overtake his mind.

The venom, it's doing something to me.

And then his world faded to black.

Jimmy didn't know what to do. His brother was doubled over in pain from the bite he had suffered, and the door still wouldn't budge. He couldn't see where Terry had gone, and there were spiders everywhere.

Alex fell over onto his back. In the dim light from Terry's flashlight Jimmy could see the pain on his brother's face.

"Jimmy, help me," Alex moaned.

A foot-long spider, brown and black and bristling with agitated movement, crawled across his face, pausing just long enough to stab his cheek with its fangs.

Jimmy grabbed Alex by the leg and pulled with all his might. He fell back against the wall when strings of webbing, some bigger than his wrist, streamed down from above and latched onto Alex, yanking his body up with one swift jerk. Alex hung there like a human puppet for several incredibly long seconds and then danced down the hallway, disappearing into the same room where Terry was.

Jimmy spun around, and with renewed strength he did know he possessed, pulled on the door for all he was worth.

This time however, it opened, just a crack, just enough to tease him with a chance of survival.

He dug his fingers into the one-inch gap he had created between the door and the frame and pulled even harder. He could only hope that nothing bit him.

The door creaked open another inch, and then a few more. Sticky sheets of webbing clung to the door and the frame in a vain attempt to keep the door closed, but was gradually giving way.

With one final tug, the door flung open. It smacked into the wall with silent force, cushioned by the webbing covering it.

Outside, the early evening rushed into the house, washing over Jimmy with its promise of escape. He was going to make it, although his excitement at the prospect of survival was diluted substantially by the fact that he was going to abandon his brother and friends.

But what choice did he have? He was just a kid. He was no match for whatever supernatural forces were at work in the house. He couldn't fight powers that he didn't understand.

"I'll be right back!" he shouted down the hallway. "I'm going to go and get help. You guys be strong. I'll be back with the police."

The house swallowed his flimsy words.

Jimmy turned and raced out of the house. He ran as fast as he could, never once looking back. He feared if he did he'd see the spiders coming after him.

He ran a few hundred feet before coming to an abrupt and jarring stop. He straightened up and closed his eyes as tightly as he could. A feeling of defeat overcame him then, one that he couldn't deny. He'd never be able to get away from them: the spiders, the house, the evil dwelling there, and he knew it.

Reaching a trembling hand back over his head, he felt around until he touched it.

The thick strand of webbing stuck to his fingers like glue.

He stretched his hand lower and brushed across another strand. He moved over to his right shoulder, and then his left, finding more threads in each spot. His breath froze in his throat and his knees buckled, but he didn't fall. Instead, the webbing jerked him upright, forcing him to stand, and then began to pull him backward.

Back to the house.

Jimmy was helpless. All he could do was twist his head back just enough to see the house as he drew closer and closer to it.

He saw three figures standing on the front porch.

Brad, Terry, and Alex were waving at him, gesturing for him to come inside. Their feet dangled above the warped floorboards of the porch; their bodies were suspended by webbing. They wore blank expressions, much like puppets, and jostled back and forth as the manipulators, the spiders pulling the strings, worked their magic.

~ 90 ~

Jimmy's feet skidded up to the porch.

Brad, Terry, and Alex were pulled into the house ahead of Jimmy. Each said nothing, and moved with the same detached machinations of a robot.

Jimmy followed his brother and friends. The spiders worked feverishly to shift him into position, and for the most part they succeeded. Only his fingers twitched out of place.

The door slammed shut just as Jimmy crossed the threshold. A sheet of webbing sealed it, allowing the spiders privacy from the outside world. They had four new acquisitions to deal with, and needed time to prepare them for any future victims who might stumble into their lair.

The Mother

Tara fell to the floor. The machete, a half-dulled piece of scrap metal that she had managed to scavenge from an abandoned warehouse, felt good in her hand. Despite the dire situation she was in it still gave her a feeling of power. She could wield it with the best of them, swinging it with deadly accuracy.

More than once it had saved her life.

The knife weighed down her one hand, a scratched and well-worn walkie-talkie her other. A red dot on its façade indicated that there was power, however weak.

Tara brushed a strand of tangled black hair out of her face and raised the receiver to her lips. She cleared her throat in nervous anticipation. If Larry didn't answer that might mean he was in trouble, or worse.

She cringed at the thought of it.

Terrible images of Larry wrapped in a dense sheet of webbing, basketball-sized spiders scurrying this way and that, jabbing him with their venom-filled fangs, flitted across her frightened and weary mind.

He hadn't checked in with her like he was supposed to. She had no idea how long it had been (time had lost all meaning since the invasion began), but she knew it had been too long since he had called her.

Way too long.

Sweat coated her forehead. She couldn't remember the last time she had a shower, much less washed her hair or wore clean clothes. Personal hygiene had become of secondary importance since the invasion had started. It, like most other aspects of comfort or pleasure, just didn't seem to matter much anymore.

What did matter however was survival.

The spiders, or whatever they were, had taken over most of the cities and were now threatening rural areas as well, gradually spreading their filth like the plague.

Tara took a deep breath and pressed the button on the side of the walkie-talkie. A sharp beep echoed in the room, indicating that she could talk into it.

"Larry, are you there? Come in. Larry?"

The words seemed to roll out of her mouth and dropped to the floor. They were laced with worry and fear.

She waited with bated breath for a reply.

"Larry, come in. Are you all right? Larry?"

After half and half a minute of agonizing silence, Larry finally answered.

"Yeah, Tara, I'm here."

Tara felt the breath return to her body.

"Thank God! Where are you? Why didn't you check in?" She hated to nag him but they were living in dangerous times. It had been nearly six months since the spiders had drifted down from the sky, seemingly from the clouds themselves, and she remembered it so well that it's still dictated every move and decision she made.

A brief silence ensued, punctuated by annoying static.

"Sorry about that, Tara, but I think I found something."

Tara's stomach grumbled.

Did he find food? Or fresh water? Or maybe some medical supplies? Even a magazine or two would be a welcome addition to their meager supplies.

As long as the spiders hadn't gotten to it first, that is. When they did they made it obvious that they possessed at the very least some type of rudimentary intelligence. They spoiled food with excrement, ruined the water or other drinkable liquids with their digestive juices (that's what she assumed it was anyway) and even tore up or otherwise destroyed books, magazines, or anything that people would enjoy. It was as if they weren't just seeking prey for sustenance, but wanted to torture them as well.

"What? What did you find?"

Larry mumbled something into the receiver. Tara's struggled to make sense of it. She could only understand a few sparse words.

Big, mother, chasm, endless, and hissing was all she could make out.

"Larry, you have to speak up. I can't hear what you're saying."

"I… I can't. It's moving again. It's turning toward me. I can see it in the green glow."

"What is? What's moving? What green light?"

Larry fell silent again, but started talking after a minute or so. "It's the mother, and she's big, at least ten feet high, maybe more. The legs are the size of a man, and she's laying eggs. They're sliding out of her like crazy. It's a real nightmare."

The words hit Tara like a kick in the gut. The image that her mind conjured up nearly caused her to fall to the floor.

"The mother?" She couldn't believe (or didn't want to) the sheer magnitude of what Larry was saying. "What is it? Would do you see?"

Larry grunted a little as he adjusted his position. "A spider, Tara, it's a freaking spider! But one the size of a house! There's other ones around it too, surrounding it. Hundreds, maybe thousands. And this strange green light is everywhere."

Tara took a deep breath to steady her nerves. "All right, listen to me, Larry," she said into the receiver. "I want you to get out of there. Do you hear me? Get out of there now."

Larry didn't answer for what felt like hours.

"Oh my God," he breathed into the walkie-talkie. "I don't believe it."

"What? What is it?"

"People, Tara, there's people in there. The mother, that thing, has people that it's…"

"What? Tell me, Larry!"

"It's… it's doing something to them, mating with them."

Tara's heart skipped a beat. Her stomach knotted up. Her head spun around the room. She struggled to speak. "Are you sure?" she finally spit out.

"Oh God yes I'm sure. That thing is mating with them. I don't know how it's doing it, but it is."

~ 96 ~

"Get out of there now!"

Larry nodded, clicked off his walkie-talkie, and began to sneak back the way he came. He could only hope that the path was still clear. If the spiders had found the opening he'd made to gain entry into the barn, then he'd be as good as dead.

He moved slowly, cautiously, being exceedingly careful not to bump into anything.

And then he felt it: a spray of something dense and sticky, something that covered his entire body with its cumbersome embrace.

The web stuck fast to every part of him. It wrapped around his hands, his feet, his legs, even his head, effectively prohibiting him from moving.

He was trapped, a sitting duck in a pond rimmed with hunters.

Larry's gun, a small-caliber pistol he'd come across in a back alley shortly after the spiders had landed, was still in his hand, his finger resting on the trigger. He couldn't move his hand or finger though, so it was therefore useless to him.

"Do you have him?" thin, raspy voice said from the shadows.

Larry managed to crane his neck just enough to see who was talking.

It was a man. He was tall and imposing and was standing about ten feet away, in the shadows.

Larry couldn't see his face.

Two other men were crouched down on either side of the man, each holding out their arms, palms up. One of them then tensed and Larry was sprayed with another jet of webbing.

"We have them now," the tall man said.

The tall man crept forward. He moved in a seamless, unnatural way.

Larry strained to see through the webbing that covered his face. All he could make out were vague figures moving around him. Some were small (no bigger than a child), while others were the size of a fully-grown adult.

The largest was the tall man, who stood in the background, apparently directing the others.

Larry tried to cry out when he felt something puncture his leg, but only succeeded in pushing out incoherent groans. He immediately felt an all-encompassing pain envelope him, but could do nothing to alleviate it.

The spider scuttled away into the shadows.

With his head swimming because of the venom coursing through his body, Larry passed out. And before darkness overtook him, he heard the tall man say: "Let's get moving. Mother will want him while he's still fresh."

*   *   *   *

Tara could only stare at her walkie-talkie. It felt like a poisonous snake in her hand.

Feeling helpless, she forced herself to calm down. Panicking would do no good. It wouldn't help her situation at all. She needed to be rational.

"I have to call Larry," she said to herself. "He hasn't called me back because he's sneaking out of wherever he's at." Somehow by saying the words to herself they seemed to be more reassuring.

An image of a ten-foot tall spider doing God-only-knows what to its prisoners ran across her mind.

"He got out in one piece. I know he did. He found some food and water and medicine and is on his way back here now."

Tara raised the walkie-talkie to her mouth, but hesitated.

My voice could give his location away. I have to wait for him. He'll be back here any minute.

Movement caught her attention.

She flung her head to the side and brandished her machete as if it were the most elegantly fashioned blade in the world.

A spider. It was only a spider. Somewhat large, with alternating bands of brown and black hairs on its legs and abdomen, but just a spider nonetheless.

Only a spider.

Tara dropped her weapon to her side and leaned in close to her small companion. She watched it warily, noting how it seemed poised to flee if she made any sudden movements.

"You're not the one doing all this, are you?" she said. "You're from Earth, born here naturally, not from some giant, egg-laying monster."

She felt foolish for speaking her thoughts, but it helped her feel better. She wasn't sure how, but it did.

The spider curled its legs under its body and settled down in its web. Its tiny head tilted to the side ever so slightly as if it understood the human speaking to it.

Its fangs twitched.

Tara spun around. She still held her machete, but it felt useless to her now. What was the sense of going on if Larry was gone? How could she continue the struggle by herself?

A knock on the door startled her from her thoughts.

Larry?

Another knock, this one harder, more forceful.

"Larry? Is that you?"

"Open up, Tara. It's me. Hurry. I think they're following me."

Tara felt as if the weight of the world were lifted off her shoulders. She rushed to the door, slid the deadbolt mechanism over, and twisted the lock. The door was pushed inward at breakneck speed, nearly knocking her over in the process.

She narrowly missed injury.

Larry stumbled into the room. He was out of breath and his face was flush from exertion. He was sweating profusely.

"Oh my God, Larry!" Tara exclaimed and hurriedly locked the door behind him.

Larry fell into a chair and ran his hands over his face. "I got out. I got bit though." He gestured to his leg. "But I cut the poison out. I'm all right now."

Tara spread the torn strips of fabric out of the way to reveal a pair of angry red and black punctures and a jagged slit down the middle. Swollen flesh surrounded the wounds and milky-clear fluid oozed from each site.

"I managed to clean most of it out, but you have to finish it. You have to hurry. I'm feeling a lot of pain."

Tara nodded, and without a word, bent over and used her mouth to suck the remaining venom out. A sickly-sweet taste caused her to gag, and she immediately spit the poison onto the floor.

Larry relaxed. "Thanks. That did the trick. I feel better already."

Tara wiped her mouth on her sleeve and looked at Larry. "What happened? How did you escape?" She watched him for his reaction, just to be sure. If he really was bitten by one of the spiders there'd be no telling what kind of side effects he could have.

Larry stood up. He was weak but managed to support himself by leaning against a table. "Well, as I said, I found their nest, where the queen is, their mother." His face tightened at the recollection. "She was horrible. Ten feet high, maybe more. There were thousands of spiders attending her.

They were scampering every which way. There were people there too, men who were wrapped up in silk with only their faces open.

I saw them, Tara. They were still alive."

Tara wiped a tear from her eye. The anguish she felt for her fellow human beings was overwhelming.

But it was also tempered by anger. These spiders, these creatures thought they could come here and take over the world, but they were wrong. She'd show them they were wrong. One way or another, she would show them.

Tara stood up and stepped over to a window. "All right then," she said with determination. "We have to stop this now." She looked out the window at the barren landscape that surrounded the building. "I'm going to load up with weapons and find that thing. Do you remember where it was?"

Larry nodded. "Yeah, about two or three miles from here, North, near the highway. Just follow the road until you reach a fork and then go right. You'll see it, an old barn, faded so much it looks gray. She's in there, down below ground."

Tara smiled. Confidence swelled in her. She knew she could do it. She knew if she was quick and quiet, she'd be able to find the monster, plant a couple of pipe bombs right under its nose, and get out of Dodge before it knew what hit it.

And even if she didn't make it out alive, she'd at least be saving the world.

Of course that was assuming there was only one mother spider.

"I'll do it," she announced, and immediately began packing a bag with food, water, and weapons. "How many bombs do we have left?"

Larry walked up to her and wrapped his arms around her. "I want to go too. I'll be strong enough by morning, and then we'll head out." He kissed the back of her neck. "I care about you, Tara. It'll be safer if we both go."

Tara knew what he said made sense, but also knew that the longer the mother had to procreate, the less chance of survival mankind would have. There'd be thousands, perhaps millions of those spider things roaming around the countryside in no time at all.

No, she had to act quickly. She couldn't wait until morning.

"Larry, I care about you too," Tara said. A knot formed in her gut. "But I'm going now, alone. I can take care of myself. Stealth is more important than strength in this situation. I need to sneak in quickly and quietly. I'll get close to the mother and detonate as many bombs as I can." She grit her teeth to maintain her composure. It wasn't easy.

She turned and walked over to where they kept supplies of weapons. She rummaged through them until she found the pipe bombs

Larry had made when they first set themselves up in the building. She grabbed the explosives and stuffed them into a tattered backpack, along with a few bottles of water, several packages of saltine crackers and two pieces of mostly-stale bread.

Larry pulled himself upright and managed to make his way over to Tara.

"Please, Tara, if we both go, it'll be safer. I know the way. I know where she is. I know how to get inside and how to get out again. You need me. We need each other."

"No," Tara retorted angrily. "What you need to do is stay here and rest." She pushed past him and walked over to the door. She held the backpack in one hand and her machete in the other. A small-caliber pistol was tucked in her waistband, and a pair of worn leather gloves hung out of her back pocket.

She was ready to save the world.

She felt it before she saw it: a tangled mass of sticky webbing that enveloped her head.

Panic seized her mind.

She flailed her arms around, dropping the backpack in the process, in a desperate attempt to free herself from her entanglement.

And then, as if to magnify the fear and confusion that was strangling her, a voice, a familiar voice, one she recognized, called out to her.

"Tara, I can't let you go."

The words hurt her more than the spiders ever could.

She clenched her hands into fists and turned her head enough to see Larry.

He was standing ten feet behind her. His face was contorted into a mockery of being human. His eyes were no more than black, soulless slits. His skin was ashen and pock- marked with web-ridden soars.

"You're not going anywhere."

Tara opened her mouth to speak but only managed to utter gibberish. She wanted to ask Larry what in heavens name he was doing, but there was no need. She already knew.

She saw the webbing trailing down from his wrists.

Larry tensed his arms, and with a grunt of satisfaction, shot another blast of webbing at Tara. It sailed through the air at incredible speed, spiraling straight toward her with deadly accuracy.

Tara managed to fall to the side and avoid any more of the substance. She rolled over and was able to grab her machete and cut herself free from her silky bounds.

"We will decimate this puny planet."

"Larry! Stop it!"

"Mother will spread her young to all corners of this…

"Shut up!"

Tara bolted to her feet and made for the door. She fully realized that she should have killed Larry, to put him out of his misery if nothing else, but couldn't. She cared too much about him. It would have torn her heart in half to hurt him, regardless of the pitiful and dangerous condition he was in.

So she ran. She just grabbed the backpack, turned around, and ran for all she was worth. In her mind she hoped and prayed that if she did succeed in destroying the mother spider that somehow, someway that would return her victims back to normal people again. Just like vampires. Kill Count Dracula and his minions would be normal once again.

It worked in books and movies, so why not now?

Behind her she could hear Larry howling in rage. He shot more strands of silk in her direction but they missed their target.

When Tara was far enough away she ducked behind a copse of trees. She had to catch her breath. She needed to gather her thoughts and go over her plan of attack.

"All right," Tara," she panted between sobs. "Larry is gone. You need to stick to your plan: find the barn, locate the mother spider, and blow her to kingdom come."

She sighed. "Piece of cake."

Catching a glimpse of movement in her peripheral vision, Tara turned just in time to see Larry coming at her. He was on all fours, crawling across the ground like some homicidal lunatic. His limbs were multi-jointed, bent at painfully- impossible angles, and Tara could hear the sickening cracks and pops over his growls.

"Did you hear what I said earlier?" he asked in an eerily-familiar voice. "I said you're not going anywhere."

Tara could see the spiders that were gathering around Larry. Dozens of beasts of varying sizes and colors were crawling alongside him, joining in the hunt.

She pulled out her machete and instinctively flung it at Larry. She then closed her eyes as tightly as she could, not being able to bear the sight of his death.

The blade sliced into Larry's neck, cleanly severing his malformed head from his body.

He collapsed in a lifeless heap.

The spiders then rushed forward. The two in the lead were huge creatures, each measuring two feet across, perhaps more. Both had downward-curved fangs of pure white that contrasted sharply with their jet-black hides.

Behind them, hissing in a horrendous symphony, were a dozen other spiders. Each had leg spans of several inches and sported eyes the size of marbles.

They trained them on Tara.

Tara leapt to her feet, ignoring the fatigue that was threatening to force her to her knees, and stumbled away from the approaching monsters. As she did so she managed to light one of the pipe bombs and hurled it behind her. Her agility and presence of mind in the face of such horrors surprised her, and she couldn't help but let out a shriek of triumph when the explosive detonated and scattered the spider's bodies in all directions.

"Take that!" she cried.

When her satisfaction diminished Tara realized that she had made a lot of noise. She quickly scanned the surrounding landscape, and seeing that it was clear, continued on her journey.

The barn was easy to find. It stood mostly by itself, with only a few long-forgotten pieces of farm equipment and a small house the size of a trailer scattered around its imposing presence.

Tara immediately set to work. She found a spot between a few old tractors and rummaged through her bag until she found the two remaining pipe bombs and a pistol. She tucked the gun, along with her trusty machete, into her waistband, and held both bombs in her hand. She then fished out a bottle of water, took a large drink, and put it back in the bag. Her lighter was easy to find; she had kept it in her pant pocket. If she lost it she'd have no way to light the bombs.

Then she'd be a sitting duck.

A strange and unsettling thought occurred to her then: *What did they do with female victims?*

Brushing off an icy shudder, Tara left the relative sanctuary of her hiding spot.

She crept up to the side of the barn. It seemed solid enough. There were no openings of any kind to be seen. She thought about simply pulling a few of the planks off, but decided not to. It would undoubtedly make too much noise. She couldn't afford to lose her most powerful weapon: surprise. If the spiders knew she was there they'd surely swarm and easily overtake her.

She crawled along the ground, always holding onto the bombs. She was scared to set them down, even for a minute. She needed to have them in her hands at all times. Without them she'd be in an even worse predicament.

Fortunately, she eventually found the spot where Larry had made a way inside the barn. It was small, no more than two planks wide, but it would have to do. If he managed to get through it so could she.

She squeezed through the opening with only an inch of clearance on each side.

Once inside the barn, Tara made her way along a long depression in the ground, most likely caused by years of drainage from rain, and followed a strange glow that seemed to come from beneath the dirt itself. It was pale green in color and was just enough to light her way.

It was then that she realized she had forgotten to bring a flashlight.

She noticed that the glow was most concentrated in a far corner near a row of ramshackle stalls. She crawled over to the area and was shocked when one of her hands sank into the soil, revealing a hidden tunnel that stretched deep underground. It snaked to her left, went on for five or six feet, and then trailed out of sight. She quickly widened the hole as much as she could.

Wondering why there were no spiders lurking about, Tara took a deep breath and crawled into the hole.

After a few dozen feet the tunnel expanded into a yawning chasm that stirred with movement. Hundreds of spiders of every color and size squirmed it one giant dance of mindless abandon. And within the seething maelstrom of thrashing fangs and gyrating limbs, at its center, was a huge mass that moved in a slow, almost hypnotic way, swinging its many legs back and forth, up and down, forward and backward.

Tara was splayed out on the ground. She watched helplessly as the giant beast was attended to by its minions. They crawled all around it, cleaning its bloated body and snatching away remnants of past meals.

The mother of spiders, the size of a small house and infinite in her ferocity, held court over her subjects.

Near her were others as well, humans, males who were being handled in ways that suggested…

"Oh God no," Tara whispered.

She felt the weight of the pipe bombs in her hands.

Let's do this. Kill that thing before it gets a chance to create more. Kill it now.

A small spider lowered itself down from a single strand of silk and landed on Tara's hand. It sensed what the bombs were and what they were capable of. With all its strength it dug its tiny fangs into her flesh and attempted to pump its potent venom into the wounds.

But Tara reacted quickly and swatted it away.

It knows why I'm here.

Realizing her tight window of time, Tara flicked her lighter until a strong flame danced at its tip and held it up to the wicks of the bombs. Instantly they ignited, further imploring her to hurry.

At that moment, several cat-sized spiders crawled toward her. Their soulless black eyes reflected the greenish glow of the scene and amplified their ominous intent.

Tara screamed and threw both bombs with all her might at the thing squatting in the center of the underground chamber. She didn't have time to think. She had to act quickly, otherwise she might not get another chance.

The pipe bombs sailed through the air in slow motion. It seemed to take forever for them to finally land with a sickening thud on their target. One hit the mother squarely on her abdomen and became lodged between the dense, coarse hairs on her body, and the other smacked into one of her legs, bounced off, and rolled directly under her, finally coming to rest beneath her head.

Tara ignored the approaching spiders. Her attention was focused on the bombs. She had to make sure they didn't go out, then she'd make a hasty retreat and hopefully get out of the building alive.

The bombs ignited simultaneously. Two brilliant yellow flashes filled the cavern with life-shattering heat and power. Scores of spiders were scattered, popping like eggs on a hot sidewalk, obliterated in the instant it took for their relatively fragile bodies to be torn apart.

The mother was killed instantly. Her head was blown apart by the blast and her abdomen was cleaved in half, both sides falling to the wayside, exposing the intricate workings of some awful, distant deity.

And the men in the chamber, the poor souls who were being used by the abomination, squirmed as their lives were extinguished. They fell apart in the blasts like so many flowers in a hurricane, utterly destroyed and forever wiped from the face of the Earth.

But not all the spiders were killed. There were still the ones crawling toward her.

Tara looked up from her disorientation from the explosions and came face-to-face with the beasts, all seven of them, each hissing in rage over the loss of their queen. Behind them was a terrible wasteland, a post-apocalyptic painting, a gore-infested graveyard of otherworldly proportions. Nothing moved there. Nothing lived.

Despite her mind being hazed over and her ears still ringing, Tara thought quickly. She sat up and fished the machete out with one hand and the pistol with the other. Four quick shots ended the lives of three of the spiders, and a vicious attack with the blade took down two more, cutting them to gory ribbons.

The two remaining spiders charged forward, fangs gnashing, eyes filled with ravenous bloodlust.

Tara reared back her machete, deferring the more effective pistol to backup status, and brought the blade down on one of the spider's heads, splitting the bulging cranium of the creature into two halves.

Dark-blue brain matter oozed out of the gaping wound.

The last spider leaped over its fallen comrade. Its fangs extended outward like a pair of steak knives.

Tara yanked the machete from the remains of the dead spider and sliced it through the air in a sideways motion. It struck the beast between its head and abdomen, neatly decapitating her crawling adversary.

A deathly silence settled over the scene. In a way it was worse than the sounds of the spiders. Somehow it seemed all the more unnatural, uncomfortable, dangerous.

She pulled the blade from the carcass and smiled. She was pleased with herself. She'd won. She'd completed her mission and destroyed the queen, stopping it from creating more of its offspring.

She gathered her things and crawled out of the hole. Once she reached the warehouse she would pack up what she could and leave, searching for other survivors, and hopefully avoiding any more spiders.

But a nagging thought tempered her weary enthusiasm: *Was that the only queen?*